MY LITTLE SISTER ATE ONE HARE . . .

by Bill Grossman • illustrated by Kevin Hawkes

Scholastic Inc.
New York   Toronto   London   Auckland   Sydney

My little sister ate 1 hare.
We thought she'd throw up then and there.
But she didn't.

My little sister ate 2 snakes.
She ate 2 snakes, for heaven sakes!
She ate 2 snakes. She ate 1 hare.
We thought she'd throw up then and there.
But she didn't.

My little sister ate 3 ants.
She even ate their underpants.
She ate 2 snakes. She ate 1 hare.
We thought she'd throw up then and there.
But she didn't.

My little sister ate 4 shrews.
She ate their smelly socks and shoes.
She ate 3 ants, 2 snakes, 1 hare.
We thought she'd throw up then and there.
But she didn't.

My little sister ate 5 bats.
She ate their coats and ties and hats.
4 shrews, 3 ants, 2 snakes, 1 hare.
We thought she'd throw up then and there.
But she didn't.

My little sister ate 6 mice,
Then spit them out and ate them twice.
She ate 5 bats, 4 shrews, 3 ants.
She even ate their underpants.
She ate 2 snakes. She ate 1 hare.
We thought she'd throw up then and there.
But she didn't.

She captured 7 polliwogs
And ate them as they turned to frogs.
She ate 6 mice, 5 bats, 4 shrews.
She ate their smelly socks and shoes.
She ate 3 ants, 2 snakes, 1 hare.
We thought she'd throw up then and there.
But she didn't.

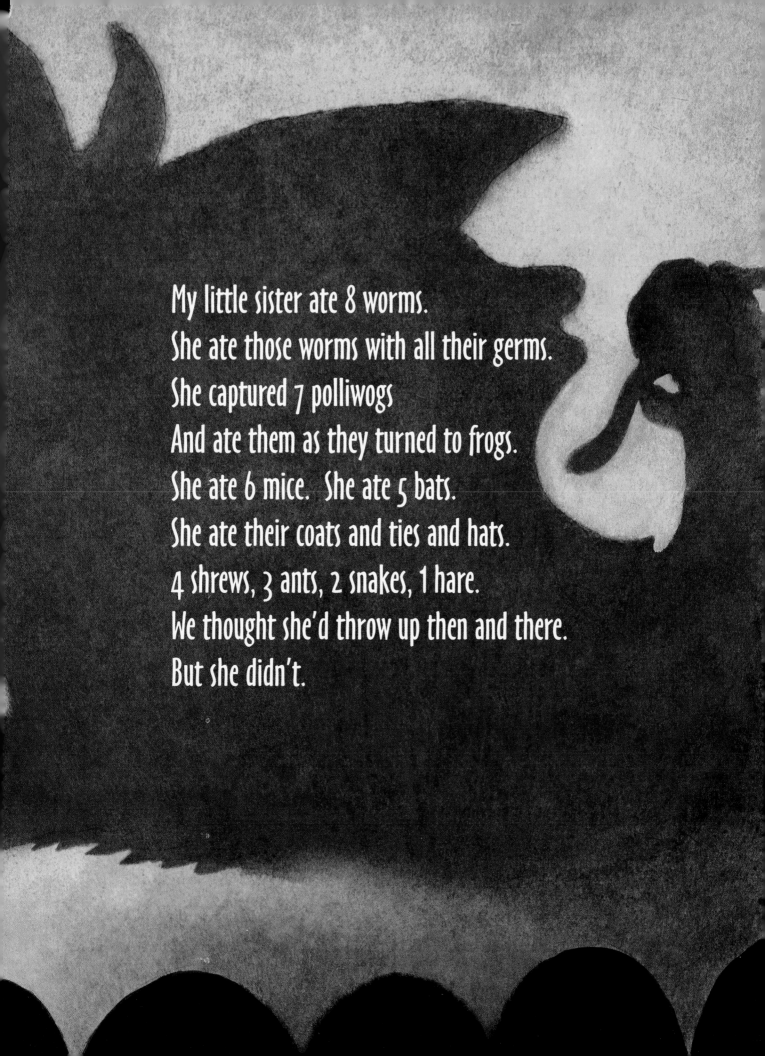

My little sister ate 8 worms.
She ate those worms with all their germs.
She captured 7 polliwogs
And ate them as they turned to frogs.
She ate 6 mice. She ate 5 bats.
She ate their coats and ties and hats.
4 shrews, 3 ants, 2 snakes, 1 hare.
We thought she'd throw up then and there.
But she didn't.

My little sister ate 9 lizards.
She ate their heads and legs and gizzards.
My little sister ate 8 worms.
She ate those worms with all their germs.
And 7 polliwogs, 6 mice.
She spit them out and ate them twice.
5 bats, 4 shrews, 3 ants, 2 snakes.
She ate 2 snakes, for heaven sakes!
And, of course, she ate 1 hare.
We thought she'd throw up then and there.
But she didn't.

My little sister ate 10 peas.
But eating healthy foods like these
Makes my sister sick, I guess.

Oh, my goodness! What a mess!

To Evelyn and Mike Anischik
—B. G.

To Jessie, who entertains us all
—K. H.

ISBN 0-590-12783-7

12 11 10 9 8 7 6 5 4 3 2 1   7 8 9/9 0 1 2/0

Printed in the U.S.A.   14
First Scholastic printing, October 1997